WELCOME TO THE

WYRD WEST

GO BEYOND LEGEND

GHOST RIDERS

Bound by the spectres of an old frontier myth, a posse must defy the forces of the Law to do what is right and go beyond legend.

BROKEN WINGS

Erica's father suffers a manic fever to build a Flying Machine, but refuses to believe that a terrifying monster lurks below their ranch.

DREAD RECKONING

Royce Falco faces his last midnight in the haunted Hayworth Penitentiary before being sent to the gallows the next morning.

HORSE NATION

The Tobin brothers, investigating unexplained phenomena, become part of an Indian ceremony that they didn't know they were destined to join.

SILENT ECHOES

The only evidence of people vanishing from Echo Station are the telegraphed messages wired to Sundown, telling of sinister plague doctors.

WYRD WEST

BROKEN WINGS

L.T. PHOENIX

Broken Wings

Published by Phoenix Forge.

Print: ISBN: 9780994642646
Digital ISBN: 9780994642622

2.2

BROKEN WINGS

"His nearness to the devouring sun softened the fragrant wax that held the wings: and the wax melted: he flailed with bare arms, but losing his oar-like wings, could not ride the air. Even as his mouth was crying his father's name, it vanished into the dark blue sea, the Icarian Sea, called after him."

– Ovid
"Metamorphoses,
Bk VIII:183-235 Daedalus and Icarus"

FOREWORD

What follows are the journal entries of patient Erica Voland as she recounts the alleged events that led to her father's apparent descent into madness, including a manic quest to build a flying machine and the discovery of a terrifying monster that dwelled in an abandoned gold mine below their ranch.

Collated by Doctor Perry Berkshire
Columbia Asylum for the Mentally Insane
La Grande, Wakoda Territory

FIRST ENTRY

"My Flying Machine will soar from the ranch by the Fourth of July!" Papa had claimed at the supper table. "And, Erica," he pointed at me, "you'll be writing everything down as I go."

Mama coughed from behind her kerchief, straining to speak. "Don't forget about the ranch." While her condition was getting worse, she still knew she had to rein Papa in whenever he had yet another idea for another crazy scheme.

"Don't worry," Papa assured, "by writing down everything about the Flying Machine, Erica's book-skills can finally be used for something useful."

"Papa..." I frowned.

"Well, you've already scared away anyone in the area that'd make a good husband by showing you can read and talk back smart. You're nineteen now, you shouldn't have your nose in books... You should be learning to be like your Mama in the kitchen."

I tried not to let my blood boil.

"You'll put it in a useful book, maybe we'll try to get one of them photographs of it, sell the Flying Machine book, make more money than the ranch has ever seen. We could sell the ranch, pack up, and with all the money we could move to La Grande and find a real nice place, find a good doctor that'll fix Mama up real nice too... You'll see."

Our property, branded by the rusting sign at the front gate as *Matthias Ranch*, had been bought years ago from the woman known across the territory as the *Gold Baroness*. Papa always says he, "Bought it for a steal." It was an opportunity too good to pass on for settlers wanting to start ranching in the West. He and Mama didn't have much to begin with and this Twyla Matthias lady was willing to part with her ranch for far less than Papa valued it at.

All on account of her husband being killed by Indians while working the ranch...

Papa just assumed that the Gold Baroness wanted to move on, leave the bad memory behind, so she didn't care for how much. Even without any livestock included, the ranch had been bought cheap.

And Papa always said, time and again, that if the Indians were going to be a problem for the ranch that he'd simply just keep all his rifles loaded in case of any hostility from them.

SECOND ENTRY

During one supper, a few days later, there came a terrifying shriek from outside the house.

It was the kind of screech that pumps your blood so much that you think you will jump out of your skin. It was piercing - so sharp, as though the sound stabbed right through your ears and into to your skull.

"Wolves?" Mama coughed.

Papa was already to a rifle leaning near the fireplace and took a lantern from the mantle. "I dunno. Don't sound like any wolves I ever heard. Maybe something new – maybe whatever got the dog..."

Despite the loss of our dog being a sore spot for us all, Papa burst out the door with the lantern already lit, holding it aloft, trying to see what was happening.

Mama and I drew closer to the doorway, seeing something scurry past - except, it *was* there and it *wasn't* there.

As Papa put the lantern down on the porch so he could take his rifle in two hands we, noticed the arrows on the dirt just before the first step of the porch.

They were Indian arrows. Three of them.

Papa waved his gun about in our small area of lit darkness. "Who goes there?" He wasn't really asking for anybody; it was more of a demand of the night to alleviate the feeling of the unknown.

Somebody was out there, though.

They lit a torch, throwing the flaming brand between us all on the bare dirt, expanding the sphere of light available in the unquiet night.

It was an Indian – no mistake! – sitting atop a well-packed horse that had striped legs.

"A friend," he responded in our language, and quite well, to Papa's question that hadn't really been a question.

Papa levelled his rifle at the Indian. "The last time you lot was here, you killed the man of the ranch. That's not going to happen again. Get the fugg out of here now."

The Indian slowly placed what must have been the bow that shot the arrows upon his horse's neck. It was an odd weapon, seemingly composed of antlers. As he held his hands up to signal surrender, we really got our best look at him.

His long hair fell about a bare chest that was painted with some sort of mural in red; three vertical strokes crossing three horizontal strokes set among three circular strokes, all evenly spaced.

Why this particular detail resonated in my mind so profoundly over any other painted marks and native decorations, I don't know, but the Indian's mural had some form of frightening beauty to it.

"I am not of the ones responsible," the Indian answered, commanding a noble countenance, "just as you are not responsible for deaths among my people when this was our land."

"No, but I don't care. I bought this land fair, even have *Uncle Sam's* papers."

Papa was taking aim. I had seen it many times before when he was shooting on the property.

Then the Indian said the strangest thing. "I have been tracking a monster over this land. It has been targeting your ranch to feed."

"*Monster?* Well, I can handle the wild animals, Indian. Nothing but some foxes and occasional wolves to worry about." He put more emphasis on aiming the rifle, ignoring the fact that something strange had killed our dog recently. "I'm going to give you to the count of three."

The Indian pointed to the arrows on the ground just near our porch steps. "This is no wild animal. Do you see blood?"

Papa was trying to be careful of any tricks, but he could also see what Mama and I could see. The crude arrow heads were splashed with silver, leaving small pools of the shining liquid on the dirt.

"Indian poison," Papa explained, convincing himself that he wasn't going to be fooled by any native nonsense.

"It is what flows through the monster. It has fled for what remains of its life into the cave on your property."

"The abandoned mine?" Papa frowned.

I had never seen an Indian up close, but I'm sure this native man was being as sincere as he could be while having a gun pointed at his head.

"If I could track it further into-

Papa fired the rifle; a warning shot inches from the Indian's hair. "Get off my land, and if I see you anywhere inside the fences of my property again... I'll shoot to kill! You and any other savages you got with you out there."

The Indian tracker steadied his bow and took his reigns, carefully, and directed his horse away. When he was almost out of the sphere of

light, he looked back directly at Mama and said,
"I am sorry, I have done all I can..."

THIRD ENTRY

The day after the encounter with *Tracker*, as my mind named the Indian, it was raining.

That didn't stop Papa exploring the abandoned mine numerous times. He said that the rain was good for keeping whatever it was inside the mine trapped in there, which should make it easier to find. Although, Papa said he'd never found any signs of the *monster*.

I still wasn't allowed in there. "It's too dangerous for a young woman that should be acting like a young lady," apparently.

All that was down there was the useless junk that Papa loved, some trinkets left behind from previous mining attempts and the ranch owner before us - anything else he had added to the hoard down there himself.

I know this because years ago Papa had a crazy hunch about finding gold down there that the previous miners may have missed. Finding gold would help the ranch's financial situation. He actually let me down there with him to prospect that one time. In the end, we only managed to find a laughable pinch of gold dust for our efforts.

At sundown, when Papa came out from exploring the abandoned mine for the last time that day, there was something different about him that I just couldn't place. He'd had another spark of inspiration – that, at least, I could determine.

Papa had become possessed by a renewed desire to invent contraptions that he'd given up on in his younger years prior to marrying Mama - besides the Flying Machine. I'm talking about things like a horseless wagon, a wireless telegraph and self-attaching horseshoes.

Despite his attention upon these multiple ideas, his main focus remained on getting his Flying Machine beyond Matthias Ranch and into the sky.

FOURTH ENTRY

She just got worse as each day passed us by.

Not even the next Doctor that Papa paid for special to come in by coach all the way from La Grande could tell us what was wrong.

"Some form of physical and mental malaise," he had said, just like the one from Rosewood and the other from Sundown.

Mama just closed in on herself more and more, keeping quiet. I think that the loss of our family dog had made her even worse. There were days where it seemed like all she did was sleep or stare into nothingness, or stare out the dark window of a night.

At the times she really did start speaking, she would talk to people that weren't there or she'd want to go for a stroll into the mine. Of course, she couldn't make it to the abandoned gold mine on her own, she needed help walking, and there was no way Papa or I were going to take her there.

Sometimes I would wake up in the night thinking that I could hear Mama stirring. She'd be talking to nothing but the night again, muttering to herself.

Other times I'd take a candle and check on her, only to find her fast asleep on the special bed Papa had constructed for her.

A few times she'd be sitting beside my bed, just looking at me. Saying nothing. I'd ask her what she was doing or what was wrong. She either wouldn't answer or she'd say something that didn't make sense.

Once, Mama's words did make some sort of sense. She said something so weird.

"They come swarming in great numbers... unwary across our web... until caught in our trap... only to become our prey..."

And that's if I heard it all correctly. But, I swear it, that's along the lines of what she said. It was strange and didn't mean anything relevant. It was like she was dreaming while awake, about flies becoming caught in spiders' webs, for some bizarre reason.

I can't blame her: she was very sick.

There were some good moments when I would wake up in the night and she would be stroking my hair, much as she had from as early as I can remember. There's a certain caress that only Mama can give. She'd always had the most graceful, slender fingers you have ever seen with the finest nails. She used to always tell me that her nails, "were the latest fashion in France."

I always described her gentle touch when she would stroke my hair as though I could actually see it: her caress felt like the golden light of a sunrise over the plains.

FIFTH ENTRY

It had reached the point now where Papa was almost completely ignoring us. Mama continued to fade, and he carried himself as though nothing were amiss.

I worked the ranch as best I could in his absence, despite him not actually being physically absent. Papa used to always give me a sermon about how ranch work isn't for little girls, young women, or wives, but he had certainly started to leave it to me, his daughter, to tend to everything herself.

Lucky, I was a good learner.

It started when I was very young, understanding words easily when Mama would read me stories. Papa always frowned upon it, so Mama would read to me from her secret collection when he was out working the ranch.

That was also when she'd usually teach me how to write, sounding out words and forming them from the alphabet. There was no way educating a girl was going to see me engaged to marry a husband, he'd reiterate. My lot in life, according to him, was to wear dresses, work inside the house and one day raise children.

I was caring for the animals well enough. The cattle were doing just fine and the horses were happy. The chickens were laying eggs and the cows were giving milk. Keeping the ranch going made sure that when traders arrived I was able to do business, even if Papa refused to come out from the mine to deal with them himself. This kept a small income and allowed me to acquire supplies we didn't produce on the ranch.

I did need help with wild animals, though. There was no way Papa had ever taught his daughter how to fire a gun.

At times when the loneliness of the endless chores was overwhelming, that's when I would miss Shep the most...

Doing all this work continuously reminded me of what an important part of the family he had been. He was a really, really, good boy. And he was skilled at keeping the foxes away. If we were lucky enough and his day's adventures had been successful, he'd even bring us home a rabbit for supper.

We lost our sweet dog only a week before the announcement of the Flying Machine. Papa didn't know what had gotten poor Shep. When he found him behind the chicken coop, there were holes in his neck and scrape marks along his scalp. It wasn't a firearm and it wasn't any animal marks Papa had ever seen before.

It wouldn't have been Tracker. The few Indians currently left in the area weren't known to do this sort of thing. From what little I've been able to find on the subject of the Wakoda that lived in the area, they eat or use mostly everything they hunt, and abhor unnecessary killing. Tracker seemed just that type too. It felt like he really wanted to help us that night.

Was the *monster* that Tracker had referred to the very thing that killed Shep? If not for Papa's actions when we met him, perhaps we could have asked.

I don't know what took you, sweet dog. But I miss you. My Shephard.

SIXTH ENTRY

When Mama died, her face was so peaceful. As though the sickness that had held her just simply let go.

I'm not sure what a funeral is supposed to feel like, as I had never been to one, but I thought it would be a celebration of the life that had been. I thought there'd be a preacher and a crowd of sad people. At least that's how they were in the books I had read.

Papa didn't want a horse-drawn hearse coming to the ranch. He also didn't want to go all the way to the cemetery in Sundown.

He wanted to bury Mama here on the ranch.

Papa was so difficult to get ready. I had to call - scream! - for him three times - down the mine tunnel! - before he finally came to the house.

When he had finally come up from the mine, he was awash with beads of sweat dripping down his face. The Flying Machine was taking all his time and energy, exhausting him - sometimes he didn't even come into the house before sundown.

When Papa came from the house for the funeral, he had at least washed up a little. He didn't wear his town hat or anything particularly fancy that he may have worn if he was visiting a church, and he didn't even carry the Bible with him.

Papa came beside the sheets that Mama was wrapped in. Stood next to the hole that I had reluctantly dug in tears because he wouldn't come from the mine to do so.

Three ravens watched from the slanting beam of a collapsing fence. Their numbers increased over the last few weeks as death approached. The black birds were quiet, observant... No flutter they made.

Papa said that Mama was better now and that he would take her down into the gold mine away from predators.

Of course she was better – she was dead! She wasn't suffering any longer. I think Papa meant to say that she had gone on to a better place.

I don't know what was wrong with the hole I had dug - after all the effort I had made digging against tears. Burying her there would have surely protected her from carrion birds and predators. What's so different down in the mine?

With a strength I didn't think he possessed, because of such exhaustion, Papa heaved Mama's body in the sheets over his shoulder, making his way down into the darkness of the sloping tunnel of the mine.

Papa had returned to that place under the ground, yet again, wasting no time at all with such trivialities as the death of Mama. It's awful that it took death to release Mama, to be finally at peace, from whatever was afflicting her. But at least she didn't have to see what was becoming of her husband.

I fell to my knees and cried after Papa had disappeared into the mineshaft.

The three ravens never left my company and neither did their crooked stares. Were they judging me, or offering sympathy?

I don't think I stood back up until the sun went down.

SEVENTH ENTRY

Papa lost himself further in his work, if that were possible. The Flying Machine had now all but consumed him. It was difficult seeing him this way.

Actually, I only saw Papa on the few times I caught him on his way to the outhouse - thank God he still had the good sense to do that! I'd have to plead with him to come inside to eat a meal and drink something. His work was going to kill him otherwise, and I didn't need to lose another parent after I had lost Mama.

But, I was beginning to understand that it was the work that was helping him to cope with the passing of Mama. And it was after the loss of Mama that I saw Tracker again.

One of the wagons that delivered supplies to us from Sundown, and bought our goods to sell in their store, drove up the road into Matthias Ranch around noon.

The driver, the man doing all the talking, had a creepy veneer about him. It wasn't just the wood toothpick sticking out from under his ugly moustache or his unwashed sweaty hair and face.

It was his eyes.

His eyes just seemed to leer at me any time they could - especially when he thought I wasn't aware of it.

The other man that rode shotgun just kept a timid expression across his face, as though if he spoke out of place he'd be in some sort of trouble.

I greeted them as they drove the horses up to the house. As they unloaded the supplies from their wagon, Creepy kept ordering Timid around by calling him, "Boy," even though the balding hair and wrinkles clearly indicated he was an elderly man.

Creepy continued to ask what my name was as though that somehow made a difference to our trading relationship. Whenever I'd decline to tell him my name or if I didn't laugh at what he thought was a witty joke, he'd tell me to give him a smile.

"Come now, I bet you got a *purdy* smile."

By the time the men had finished loading our ranch's goods for sale onto their wagon and given the correct payment, that I had to argue for because I, "was just a girl," Creepy had assumed that I must be alone. My father being in the abandoned gold mine didn't sound true enough for Creepy.

He grabbed me by the arm, commanding Timid, "Boy, stay with the wagon."

And he did - Timid did nothing but nurse his shotgun close to his chest, fearful of the other.

Creepy was an offensive brute. "Let's have that *smile* inside, shall we," he said with a cheerful sneer as he dragged me toward the house.

All I could do was scream against his rough hands as his foul odour made me want to gag. His stench was so bad that I could taste it.

It was probably useless, but I hoped that Papa could hear me.

While Timid remained in the shotgun spot on the wagon, Creepy's hand that held me by the hair was struck by an arrow! His palm was speared to a wooden post that held the porch roof up. It was his turn to scream as blood flowed down his arm.

Preceded by the rapid galloping of horse's hooves, Tracker - this time fully clothed with the addition of a shirt and hat - was speeding toward us with a lasso whirling around his head like some cowboy.

Timid's shotgun was levelled at the new arrival, but he was too afraid to pull the trigger.

Tracker just rode by the wagon and its occupant, throwing the lasso over Creepy's screaming head. In one responsive motion, he told Timid to, "Turn the wagon around and drive from here until you can no longer see this property, and never return."

Tracker then about-faced his horse and rode away with Creepy's neck in the lasso. The bloodied hand was torn from the post, the arrow left behind embedded in the wood.

Creepy howled against the rope as best he could the whole way to the border of the property. It was like he was trying to free himself from the noose of a gallows as he was dragged bodily along the unforgiving dry dirt and gravel road.

When Timid had reached the perimeter, he kept driving the wagon away along the property-bordering road. Tracker galloped alongside the speeding wagon, tying his end of the lasso to the back of the wagon so that it would continue to drag Creepy.

My assumption is that the foul Creepy was dragged by his neck and lost a lot of skin along the way until well out of sight of the ranch. Even after enduring that sort of suffering, I still can't say that I felt any sympathy for him at all.

Tracker returned, reining his horse to a halt where the outer road intersected with the road that led into the ranch.

Against everything I had heard about savage Indians, I ran toward him, wanting to offer my gratitude. Even just some thanks, a small favour - perhaps even a meal - while Papa wasn't around to scare him away again.

Tracker simply tipped his hat and flicked two fingers from the brim toward me as he rode the other direction to that of the fleeing wagon.

He had broken Papa's command to stay away, but was obeying it again now that my ordeal was over. Tracker seemed an honourable man, one that didn't require reward for a good deed. I believe that his people, surely, would also be as honourable.

I never did see the dishonourable Creepy or Timid on our ranch again.

EIGHTH ENTRY

It took some time, the incident had numbed me
to some degree, but the more it sunk in the more
I realised that I was well and truly shaken by the
delivery wagon men.

Especially, Creepy. I couldn't close my eyes
without seeing and feeling him upon me. And
sometimes I thought I could smell his foul stench
even though he was well and truly gone.

I was also so mad that Papa was nowhere
to be seen, down in the mine of course. He's
supposed to be up top, looking after the ranch
and what's left of his family - looking after me!

Night was beginning to fall when I decided
not to wait and see if Papa would come to the
house, and I wasn't going to yell for him to
come.

I wanted to tell him what had happened by going against his wishes, by entering the abandoned gold mine. If Tracker was brave enough to break Papa's rules; then I could break Papa's rules.

I made sure one of our many lanterns was full of kerosene and ready to burn. I wrapped some food up for Papa. It was some dried fruits and meats, and I knew he'd need to drink more water.

When looking into it at night, the abandoned gold mine was always scary. All manner of animals had made that place their home in the past. There was no point boarding it up as something always managed to get through. Papa never wanted to collapse it, though, because he liked the mine too much to let it go.

I had nothing to fear by going into the mine because Papa was already down there. Well, nothing to fear but his reaction.

There were cobwebs everywhere, but the path downward was relatively clear as Papa would - less and less frequently - come in and out through this sloping tunnel. There were pieces of metal strewn about, old camping gear, and random items I wouldn't be able to identify.

Once I was through all that I finally laid eyes upon Papa's contraption in a more open area of the mine in all its resplendent glory.

There it was: the Flying Machine.

It looked like a giant bird, if a bird was made of wood, metal, canvas and plucked feathers. No wonder this had taken Papa so long to make. All the parts seemed to be affixed to each other by some silver adhesive.

I saw Papa leaning over something, but it wasn't a machine part or a work bench.

It was a terrifying monster.

My skin chilled with fear, my beating heart felt as though it was being held in a clutch of claws. All the stories I knew of horrific creatures lurking in the dark and the blood-curdling nightmares they caused didn't equal the beast I witnessed. This thing, this devil in shadows, was beyond comprehension.

Tracker's word that night for the terrible thing was fitting; it really was a monster.

It was slumped against the mine wall, that much I could initially gather. I try to remember elements of its grotesque appearance properly, but I recall it differently each time. It was as though it was formed of shadows. Eyes, there were many, possibly eight. And they shone from a brilliant red to a fading pink. It had more arms and legs than I could count - perhaps they were all arms or all legs. I don't know, but Papa held one of its many hands.

Yes, hands, it had what I would consider to be hands... I do remember, very well, the hands. It's the long spindly fingers of the hands that cause me to remember them the most. I would have mistaken their sharp slenderness for knives if they hadn't have acted like fingers.

Papa twisted something in the monster and it shrieked in response. It sounded much like the noise from outside on the night that Papa declared that he was going to build a Flying Machine and launch it toward La Grande by the Fourth of July. It was an arrow that Papa was twisting... it was one of Tracker's arrows! It was embedded in the monster. I had seen, personally, just how much damage one of those arrows can do and the screaming they cause.

And there were more of them. Papa had collected the arrows from our porch steps, those used to hunt this monster, and had pierced them into the creature to keep it wounded near the brink of death.

Why didn't he just kill it?

"More!" Papa commanded. "I need to fly!"

From what I can only assume was the palm of one of the monster's many lanky hands, some sort of horrible mouth opened to secrete a silver fluid that Papa took in his own hand. He slapped some of the liquid across his mouth, devouring it like a thirsty dog that hadn't had water all day.

He then lowered his head, and the creature stroked its long fingers over his scalp – gently, just like Mama would, emitting a soft golden glow like how I always imagined her touch was if it could be seen.

Papa had that manic *fervour* in his eyes again, like he'd been struck with a million brilliant ideas at once. But he was also exhausted. He had become more exhausted every day, going beyond what any man could usually endure.

Papa threw food from a table nearby at the creature – food that I had previously forced him to take from the house.

He then dragged an almost-dead fox by its tail and dumped it in front of the monster. I knew it was still alive because I could hear a slight whimper. It must have wandered in and met its fate with Papa, but in all my life I had never seen him be cruel to an animal – this whole nightmare of a scene really wasn't like him at all.

The monster sunk rows of vicious fangs, that sparkled like glass, into the fox's body. I couldn't discern what it was doing, but it somehow gained strength through those crystalline daggers.

As life left the poor animal, the monster's eyes went a brighter red and light began to emanate from its teeth and the golden aura from the hand increased in brilliance. I think it staved off its mortal wounds, as it must have been repeatedly doing since Papa had kept it secreted down here.

Papa took the remaining silver liquid in his hand and applied it to areas of his flying machine. "Tomorrow, I will take these parts to the surface and re-assemble the Flying Machine. I will fly. No test run, just straight into the sky. In La Grande I will find a doctor that can fix whatever you have done to my mind. I'll have no further use for you, *Thing*, you *Spider*. The sky will finally be mine."

It was like a spider... The monster was so reminiscent of a spider, but at the same time it wasn't, it was like... us... *Spider* was like us...

Then I understood.

Papa and Spider had caught each other in their own webs... in their own traps. Papa was torturing this monster at the brink of death for the weird silver material and the manic ability that had overtaken his thoughts to design the Flying Machine. At the same time, Spider fed on Papa's mind and what food he threw to it in a bid to keep itself alive and keep gaining enough strength to eventually escape.

But neither of them was able to gain an advantage over the other, not until the Flying Machine was finished. That contraption was a means of escape for both; whether physically for Spider to escape Tracker outside the ranch or mentally for Papa to escape the manic hell of not being able to rest.

They needed each other to survive long enough to then escape the other's insidious trap.

I think it was when Spider saw me and I dropped the food I had brought, it's startled gaze consisting of eight red glowing eyes, that I realised all this – as though those crimson jewels had telegraphed one hundred books of knowledge into my mind in that moment.

It was also then that I realised that Spider wasn't a monster at all...

Spider was my Mama...

I thought Mama had died and her body was taken down here to be buried. How long have I not realised that Mama has been alive? She's alive and helping Papa. Why didn't he come and tell me? Had I been on my own so long that I misunderstood everything that had happened? Everything had suddenly become so hazy – was I losing my mind?

I needed to get out of the mine, just like Papa and Spider wanted to do. I was overcome by a frenzied enthusiasm to make that happen.

Nothing else mattered.

With what little strength Mama seemed to have left, she held an outstretched hand to Papa. The mouth in her palm shot a thick line of silver thread, like a long spiderweb, that stuck to Papa. Mama reeled him in as though she possessed more arms than she should. As Papa fought to resist with no strength left in his body, Mama said to him, "I have no further use for you, either... *Papa.*" She sunk her teeth into his neck just as she had the fox, eyes and teeth glowing in response. Then she stroked his head with those spindly fingers, scratching his scalp until the sharp fingers left lines of blood and the soft golden light that I always imagined emanated once more.

She dropped him, Papa so exhausted he looked as sick as Mama had before she had... died...?

"Come," Mama motioned me over, refocusing my thoughts. I didn't hear her words or see her mouth move to speak them, but it was as though I *sensed* them. "Help me, so that we may leave this place together."

And so I did.

NINTH ENTRY

The Flying Machine was beautiful.

At the first light of sunrise, Mama and I had finished dragging Papa from the abandoned gold mine to his favourite rocking chair on the porch of the ranch house. He was in a complete daze, drained by his work to the point of almost collapsing.

No matter, Mama and I would see his dream come alive.

I rested one of his rifles in his arms so that he didn't have to worry about anyone coming onto the ranch again. Papa's view overlooked the road out of the property where the Flying Machine was assembled and would take flight.

Some may have considered it ugly when we finished building it, but the contraption was a miracle of engineering and the magic of belief. It was made from a compromise of the lightest and strongest wooden beams, various canvases and a variety of bird feathers the likes of most which I had never seen before. The magic ingredient of the whole contraption was Mama's silver liquid, which held together much of the machine in important places and would power its engine into the sky.

I really was surprised that Mama had become so interested in the Flying Machine while she was down in the mine with Papa. I honestly thought she had died, but it's like she had been reborn. I wished Papa had told me about her, but it was just like him, controlling everything with his rules and how things should be. She kept tending to a wound on my neck that I couldn't remember having, but I didn't feel like it was getting any better.

I spun the propellers in opposing directions. They looked like rowing oars whirling around until they were fast enough that they became blurred discs. This started the revolutionary engine that ran not on steam, but on Mama's silver brew. Unlike the very few steam trains I had heard in my life, this small engine only emitted a quiet humming.

Knocking the logs of firewood out from under the wheels, I then jumped in front of Mama, laying down on my front, looking ahead, as the contraption rolled forward. I took the guiding rod as Mama lay on top of me, holding on behind as the Flying Machine rolled forward faster than expected.

In what seemed like no time at all, we had risen from the road out of the ranch together and were ascending toward the heavens. It was Papa's dream come true, but unlike him, Mama wanted to have me along.

I looked back at Papa. I think he raised his rifle at us, only for it to drop and fall as he slid from his chair to the porch. It may have gone off.

The Flying Machine had finally beaten him, its toll exacted. He could rest now, much as I thought Mama had.

I saw Tracker riding along our underside, coming from some unseen place, unable to keep pace with us. He was shouting something I couldn't understand - perhaps it was in his own language?

I don't know why, but he started to fire arrows at us! Some struck the underside of the Flying Machine, near the rear as though he was aiming for Mama.

Did he feel that I was in danger again?

For a moment, it did seem like we were going to fall from the sky when an arrow pierced some canvas on the wing. It was an easy fix as Mama simply caressed some of her silver balm to close the hole with her elegant fingers.

An arrow did manage to strike her and she released a shriek in response, much like that we had all heard that night when we first encountered our pursuer when he claimed to be tracking a monster. Papa had been right to be wary of native nonsense.

We were getting further skyward and gained a magnificent view, such that only those in the heavens could possibly know. We flew so far away from Tracker's sight that he had to reign his horse to give up and lower his bow. There was no way that man could track the Flying Machine or either of its passengers while they soared across the sky on such magnificent wings.

TENTH ENTRY

The Flying Machine had soared from the ranch by the Fourth of July!

The first thing I did after our unsteady - but successful! - landing outside of La Grande was hide the Flying Machine from jealous eyes amongst an area that looked like a carriage graveyard.

Mama stayed with it... to keep it safe, but not before stroking my hair in that way only she knew how.

I then made my way into La Grande as a young lady in britches instead of a dress – oh how their heads turned my way!

I found the Patent Office and forced my way to the front of the line inside, telling any who'd listen about the success of the Flying Machine. Some thought me mad; a little girl in dirty boys clothes playing around with the ideas and machines of educated men of science.

Some, though, must have seen my brilliance. Their rewards came very quickly.

First, I was escorted by a steel carriage that was driven by men in blue uniforms – they looked especially important and protected me and my ideas by brandishing rifles.

They drove me to my second reward, a new boutique artist's studio, within a complex called *Columbia Asylum*, that has a sprawling view of an active seaport and churning industrial area. It had an odd name for sure, but it housed other creative types such as myself.

It's difficult to complain about such a fine reward, but the constant mechanical noise from outside and the bars on my window spoil the indulgence. I'm told by my many surely crisp-white-uniformed servants that I'll get used to the noise and that the bars are there for my protection. It's comforting to know that they are here to look out for my needs.

During the day they remove the designer jacket that binds my arms so I can finish this journal about the Flying Machine.

And sometimes, in the darkest of nights, Mama visits and sits beside my bed. She strokes my hair with her long spidery fingers, caressing my temples, her strokes still feeling like the golden light of a sunrise over the plains.

DREAD RECKONING

Royce Falco is scheduled for execution in the Hayworth Penitentiary.

His usual confidence to slip from such situations is crushed when a mysterious visitor brings news that his demise has been orchestrated, but also brings an offer to alter his fate... the decision will come at a price.

Dread sets in as Royce's last midnight approaches in the reputably haunted prison, because at 5 o'clock they take him to the gallows post.

SPOILER ALERT!

THERE'S AN EXTRACT OVER THE PAGE.

WYRD WEST

DREAD RECKONING

L.T. PHOENIX

Dread Reckoning

Copyright © L.T. Phoenix 2021

Published by Phoenix Forge.

Print: ISBN: 9780994642653
Digital ISBN: 9780994642639

2.3

DREAD

RECKONING

"Any man's death diminishes me, because I am involved in mankind. And therefore never send to know for whom the bell tolls; it tolls for thee."

– John Donne
"Devotions Upon Emergent Occasions, Meditation XVII"

XII

"That black cat is back again, crossing the road!" Michael McLaren couldn't believe his eyes. "Our tower shift almost over; so of course something weird happens."

"What, I'd hardly call that weird," the other guard on duty answered. "You sure it's the same one, Mick?"

"I dunno, cats all look the same to me. But it's black, and it keeps crossing the Road to Hell. You never use the spyglass..." McLaren handed the small sentry telescope over. "Use the spyglass!" He shook his head again. "This is bad luck, Reed... Bad luck, I tell ya."

"Well fugg me six ways from Sunday or my name ain't John Reed; that's gotta be the same cat." He wasn't as superstitious as the other, but shared his curiosity. "Why does it keep coming back? Just sits out there, then crosses the road, disappears when we're not looking, and comes back to cross the road again. And all in the cold like that with the night falling, to boot."

"And the storm clouds coming."

"Cats hate water; it's gonna get soaked," Reed agreed as he had an idea. "You know, I reckon that its master is probably inside."

"What, one of the prisoners? It's not a dog."

"Yeah, doesn't matter, it's probably pining for its master locked behind bars inside somewhere."

"Like I said, it's not a dog: it wouldn't do that."

"Why not?"

"I dunno, cat's just don't do that." McLaren braced his hands at the edge of the sentry tower, staring out at the cat as though it would bring him answers. "Poor creepy weird muttonhead. Just keeps staring at the prison."

"I bet you two bits, Mick," Reed reached inside his penitentiary uniform for the coins, "the cat is owned by one of the prisoners inside."

The other guard looked at the coins. "I'll take that bet, 'cos it's now up to you to ask some of that filth inside if they own a black cat and try to get a straight answer from any of them." McLaren laughed, adding, "Better start with Royce Falco and Clyde Mortimer; they won't be around after 5 o'clock tomorrow," while making a motion as though he was being choked by a noose.

"Don't remind me," Reed sighed. "I'm on death-watch tonight and execution in the morning. When the fugg are we supposed to sleep?"

"Me too, I'm with you for both. Hells teeth, who made the roster?" McLaren shivered. "I hate The Hole at night, and a black cat crossing the Road to Hell doesn't help things. The cells give me the creeps, and more guards have been seeing-

"Don't say it, Mick..."

A church bell rang across the prison, the sound so loud it hurt the ears.

"Hells bells... what was that?" McLaren looked around after the tolling was finished, not realising the irony of his cuss, having never heard such a bell toll in Hayworth Penitentiary.

"You just had to mention the hauntings, didn't you?" Reed searched around from the high view of the sentry tower, already sure he'd never find what could have made such a sound. "Is there a church and bell here now since my last shift?"

"I didn't say anything about the hauntings," McLaren argued, "but you did!"

"That wasn't the gallows bell, whatever it was; it's nowhere near as loud as that..." Reed spoke what they both already knew as a coping mechanism against the strange bell that was probably going to be thought of by all the guards of Hayworth Penitentiary as another haunting of The Hole. As much as he tried to reason the strange occurrence, it didn't help the unsettling feeling that began with the black cat continually crossing the aptly dubbed road that led into the prison and the effect both the animal and the mysterious bell tolling would have on them during the night shift. "So, why's this bell tolling, who's it for?"

"It sounded like a passing bell, you know, rings like that from a church before someone... dies... There's no executions at sundown to be tolled for," McLaren added, "only the two at five o'clock in the morning for Mortimer and Falco..."

XI

The loud tolling of the unusual bell throughout the prison had unsettled guards and inmates of Hayworth Penitentiary.

All except for Clyde Mortimer. The old man found the subduing effect it had on everybody amusing.

As Royce Falco was led to the cell that he would spend his last night in, marched by guards beside the other prisoner considered by most to be a lunatic, a rat crossed their path.

Mortimer jumped from his guard's loose grip, possessing an uncanny agility despite his age and the shackles binding his wrists. With limbs like spindles, he stomped after the rat.

"Mortimer! Get back here or I'll knock you senseless again," one of the guards threatened.

Royce, as shackled as Clyde, wriggled free from his own guard's hold in the commotion and shoulder-rushed the cruel old man against some cell bars. But, to Royce's dismay, it wasn't before Clyde had managed to injure the rat, the creature squealing and limping away.

"Aww," Mortimer began, a mock face of sympathy, "did the little rat getting hurt upset the *infamous* Royce Falco?"

"If you men weren't already hanging tomorrow, I'd beat you to pulp!" Royce's guard went to reclaim his prisoner.

Royce evaded, dodging. Then with his eyes set squarely on Mortimer, he launched at the lunatic. Royce's forehead hit the front of the other's skull with such force that the back of the old man's head struck the bars of their new cells.

Clyde Mortimer just laughed as Royce's guard finally managed to grab him and keep him from attacking further. "Royce Falco, *Red Roy, Famous Rat Lover of The Hole*. They should call you Rat Roy instead!" His laughter became maniacal as the other guard brought him to his feet and told him to, "Shut the fugg up."

Falco and Mortimer were put in separate cells beside each other. These spaces were to be where they would contemplate their last hours before being hanged to death by noose the next morning.

As Mortimer's guard exited the area with the other, he said without much sympathy, "God be with you..."

Mortimer snorted. It was one of the strangest responses Royce had ever heard from the crazed man as he himself pondered the absurdness of the guard's sentiment.

Mortimer rubbed his bleeding head to see how much blood he could squeeze in his fingers. "You gonna say one of them little *Injun* prayers for the rat, Red Roy?"

"Fugg off, Mortimer, don't call me that."

"Awww, come on... Rat Roy... Alright... Royce... Say one for me."

"I wouldn't fugging waste my breath on you, that's for damned sure."

"But the guard said *God be with you* to me..." Mortimer sat with his legs huddled in his arms. "I must *deserve* a prayer."

"*God be with you?* What does that even mean to people before the gallows?" Royce looked to Mortimer, seeing the pathetic old man playing with the blood from his head wounds like a child. "You deserve nothing but the noose. You can wait for a preacher, I ain't saying fugging nothing for you. The rat deserves a prayer more than you, the poor forsaken thing, after what you damn well did to it. But not you. Never you."

"But it's just vermin, Royce."

"No, Clyde, you're vermin. That rat had more class in just its tail than you have in your whole wrinkled body."

"And they say I'm crazy? Why would you pray for a filthy rodent and not the man across your cell going to the gallows with you?"

"I dunno." Royce nonchalantly replied, rubbing his forehead where he had struck Mortimer. "Probably just another bad habit I picked up from one of my brothers."

"Fugg!" Reed dropped his bits, the coins falling through the wood floorboards of the sentry tower. "Where'd he come from?"

McLaren raised the spyglass to see. "When did he get there?"

The cat never removed itself from the area. It switched at random moments between a staunch vigil staring at the front of Hayworth Penitentiary and making unnerving crossings of the road that led into the prison, despite the great tolling of the mysterious church bell.

At some point the cat was doing neither activity, instead having its black coat scratched by the white-gloved hand of a stranger in blue.

"That's what I'm saying!"

"Yeah," McLaren said, "but I didn't see him approach."

"Neither the fugg did I." Reed explained again. "That's what I'm talking about."

"Did he just sneak up?"

"Well, where from?"

Hayworth Penitentiary, located a safe and civilised distance outside La Grande, was situated in a large valley within a high hill. A Wakoda legend told that the formation was caused by a fire that fell from the sky to the earth. This garnered the penitentiary and the hill what some considered to be a misnomer; *The Hole*, as it is known among the prisoners and workers. From the sentry tower, anyone ascending the rise over the hill and descending into the valley toward the prison should be spotted with ease a literal mile away.

And the road that led into the prison under the sentry tower was known across the territory as the Road to Hell. There was a small weathered sign almost out of sight from the sentry tower beside the road that McLaren had put up years earlier, that the Warden hadn't had removed because of the reputation it garnered the prison among criminals. The branded letters read by anyone approaching the penitentiary and often recited out loud by prisoner wagon guards to their passengers bound for incarceration:

Last Road into Hell.

The man had kneeled to the cat, but not enough to put the crisp midnight-blue trousers to the cobbled road leading into Hayworth Penitentiary. As he scratched the animal under the chin, it looked as though he spoke to it.

The stranger stood, pulling a pocket watch from his vest, checking it with a refined posture. Closing it, he stepped toward the prison entrance, the black cat remaining in place despite the approaching storm.

"We'd better alert the gate, Mick, that we have an incoming visitor," Reed stated.

McLaren looked at the sentry tower's old timepiece as some guards approached. "Ah, good. Our shift's almost up, and here comes the tower night shift. We'll just go down to the gate ourselves on our way to death-watch. I wanna know who walks alone all the way along the Road to Hell when a black cat keeps crossing it during an approaching storm!"

IX

"But, what you must ask yourselves, good sirs, is this..." There was a hanging pause as the distinguished accent drifted through the barren cell corridor like a gentle breeze. "Was the card you chose at the beginning of this simple prestidigitation really the card you had chosen at all?"

Royce heard the guards' exclamation of astonishment; he could even feel their sense of questioning awe from inside his cell.

"You got a visitor, Falco," McLaren called down the hall, then added with a humoured tone of disbelief, "says he's your *preacher*."

John Reed and Michael McLaren's curiosity about the approaching stranger paid off when they were treated to card tricks beyond belief, so much so that they agreed to escort him to see a prisoner in the exact location of where their next shift was. It was happenstance that defied convenience, McLaren chalked it up to good fortune.

Mortimer chuckled from his cell, next to Royce's. "The rat's family have come to send you straight to Hell!"

Royce's brow clenched. "That doesn't even make sense; you're the one that was cruel to it."

"Life," Mortimer screamed into his pillow, "doesn't make sense."

Royce had an idea of who was coming; someone that hadn't appeared in his life for some years. As soon as the distinguished gentleman walked in to view there was no doubt to the answer of Mortimer's question of, "Who's this, dandy?"

Royce answered. "Charles Lafayette..."

The visitor raised a finger to the brim of his wide hat as an interjection. "The One and Only, Charles Lafayette, Legendary Mysterio, Illusionist, Magician, Perceptivist, Master of Cosmology, Esoterica, Fortuna, Portentia and Mysticism..." He pulled on the brim of his hat as he gave a slight bow of acknowledgement to Mortimer.

"That's a lotta fugging turd words, mister."

"Charming..." Lafayette turned to face the other prisoner.

Royce smirked. "So, how did you work your way into the restricted area that the guards call death-watch?"

"Simple tricks," the magician nodded his head back at Mortimer, "appease the simplest of minds."

"I'll fugg you up," Mortimer tried to rattle the bars of his cell, "you dandy Creole!"

Lafayette returned to the wiry old man, twirling his moustache with thought, his azure gaze piercing. "Execution at the noose is too simple of an escape for the sins you have committed, Clyde Mortimer, but there's a special place after the gallows where there is no escaping from what you did to that little girl at Rosewood..."

Royce couldn't believe it. He'd never seen Mortimer shut down like that. The man was without remorse, and no amount of reasoning could ever silence him. Only beatings by guards to the point of unconsciousness had any effect. Lafayette had somehow plucked just the right thread to unravel the lunatic, Mortimer weaking at the knees to almost fall to the floor, his wrinkled skin looking as though he'd spent a night out in the cold.

Lafayette came back to Royce's cell, those azure eyes gazing through the vertical bars at the prisoner. The man once known as Red Roy didn't know what to make of the magician's visit, but he knew such an appointment was never to be taken lightly. Royce didn't know what to say, but tried, "It's been a while, Chu-"

Royce paused as the magician's brow raised, rethinking his naming, "-arles..."

Charles Lafayette nodded, Royce seeing a small, satisfied smile across his lips. Then the magician delivered mysterious words in the manner he was known for – by the few that did know him well enough for that.

"This is where it all ends. As the evening passes and a storm of liberation descends upon Hayworth Penitentiary, you, Royce Falco, will face your last midnight."

Royce swallowed. "Grim tidings, Lafayette."

"Indeed." The magician continued. "You will also confront your brothers and your last chance at redemption. One of these brothers, in particular, has seen to it that your execution is scheduled alongside *this*"- he was referring to Mortimer - "so that it may go unnoticed by your father of whom you are used to delivering your salvation against the Law."

"Kayne..." Royce knew it.

"The very same." Lafayette acknowledged. "The man that would be king among the Falco dynasty. Kayne Falco, he who vies with you for the coveted position as the Seventh Son of a Seventh Son."

"So why don't you use one of your magic tricks to spring me from this prison so Kayne doesn't get his way?"

"Your Doom is upon you, Royce Falco," Lafayette explained. "All the powers of the universe move in cohesion so that you face the reckoning of one last midnight. You must choose redemption or death as your Fate."

"Then I choose redemption! As if I'd choose anything else..."

"Redemption, my dear Royce, isn't simply a matter of uttering a succession of traditional words – no, not at all, that won't do, that form of tyranny just will not do. You'll need to tell *them* of your decision and mean it, because they can see right through any deceit."

"Who... Tell who?" Royce was wary.

"You'll know when the time is upon you. There's many who still linger beyond death in Hayworth Penitentiary, and *they* are coming tonight..."

GHOST RIDERS

The Civil War is over. American expansion pushes westward across the United States, unaware of the supernatural dangers that lurk in the Wild West.

A Bostonian tourist is thrust against his will into this savage land of outlaws and desperados. Finding allies in a war veteran, a native tracker, a gold rush baroness, a mysterious magician and a trusty dog, Jacobi Nicholson will find that he is destined to heal some of the scars this unforgiving landscape has given his new friends.

Bound by the spectres of an old frontier myth, will the gang defy the Law to do what is right and go beyond legend...?

BROKEN WINGS

Erica's father wasn't aware of the terrifying monster that lurked below their ranch in the abandoned gold mine.

If he had known, he may not have announced that he was going to build a Flying Machine by the Fourth of July. He may not have worked on the contraption with such a manic fever, oblivious of his dying wife. And, he may have been able to avoid the monster feeding on what was left of his fragile mind.

For Erica's father, the Flying Machine and his quest for the sky had to succeed - nothing else mattered!

HORSE NATION

Matteo and Nickolas Tobin have spent years using their career as surveyors to fund their side project of investigating supernatural phenomena across the Wild West.

A native Wakoda ritual that the brothers stumble upon while exploring the area of Otter Creek will change them forever when they discover that the forces of Fate had destined them to be participants in the ceremony.

Whether Matteo and Nickolas will accept their role in that destiny is another matter.

SILENT ECHOES

An entire train and its passengers have mysteriously vanished from Echo Station overnight without a trace.

The only clues to solving the impossible occurence arrive in the form of a series of increasingly frantic messages that were telegraphed to the town of Sundown during the night of the vanishing. Descriptions abound of sinister men in beaked masks and heavy cloaks that the sender names as plague doctors, and monsters that remain unnamed.

With only the raving telegraphs as evidence, this may be an investigation that can't be solved.